Reeds dir
0800 0969 440

GW00373874

Jazz and Blues Greats for Saxophone

Wise Publications
London/New York/Sydney

Exclusive Distributors:

Music Sales Limited
8/9 Frith Street,
London W1V 5TZ, England.

Music Sales Pty Limited
120 Rothschild Avenue,
Rosebery, NSW 2018,
Australia.

This book © Copyright 1991 by Wise Publications
Order No.AM82298
ISBN 0.7119.2467.8

Designed by Pearce Marchbank Studio
Arranged & compiled by Robin De Smet
Music processed by Seton Music Graphics Limited
Cover photograph by Julian Hawkins

Printed in the United Kingdom by
Caligraving Limited, Thetford, Norfolk.

Angel Eyes

Words by Earl Brent
Music by Matt Dennis

Slowly

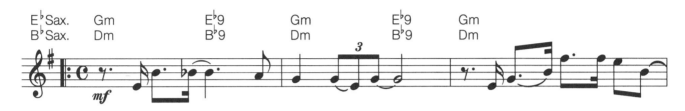

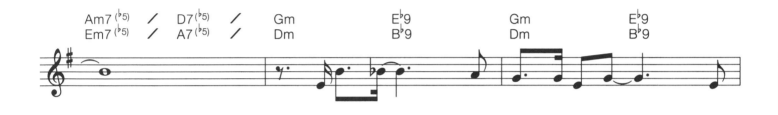

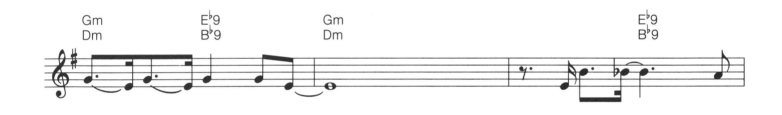

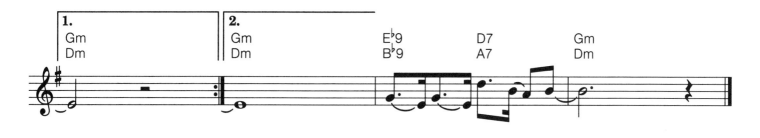

5

Baby Won't You Please Come Home

Words & Music by Charles Warfield & Clarence Williams

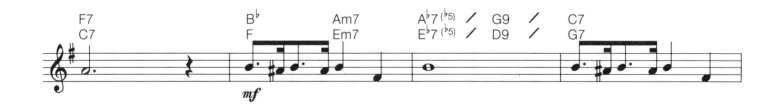

Bill Bailey Won't You Please Come Home

Traditional

Brightly

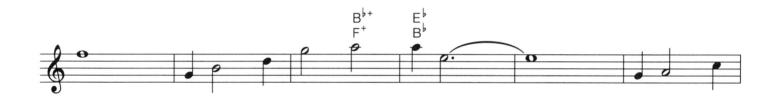

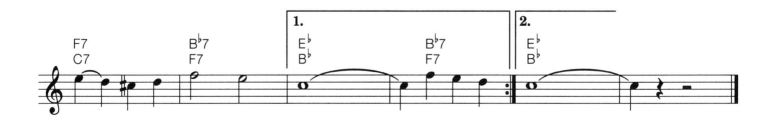

East Of The Sun (And West Of The Moon)

Words & Music by Brooks Bowman

Black Coffee

Words & Music by Paul Francis Webster & Sonny Burke

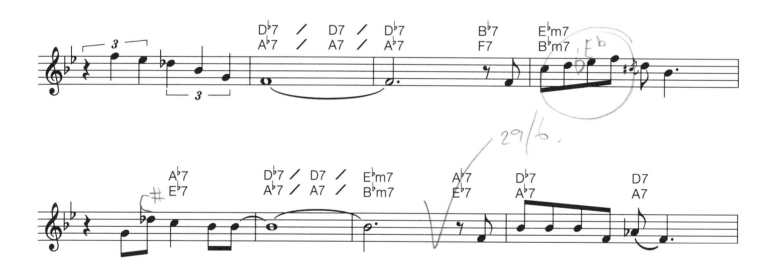

Boogie Woogie Bugle Boy

Words & Music by Don Raye & Hughie Prince

Medium Boogie Woogie

Farewell Blues

Words & Music by Elmer Schoebel, Paul Mares & Leon Rappolo

poco rit.

14

Sweet Sue—Just You

Words by Will J. Harris
Music by Victor Young

Moderato

Flying Home

By Benny Goodman & Lionel Hampton

AABA
8 8 8 8

Get reed number telephone

20/10

Honeysuckle Rose

Words by Andy Razaf
Music by Thomas 'Fats' Waller

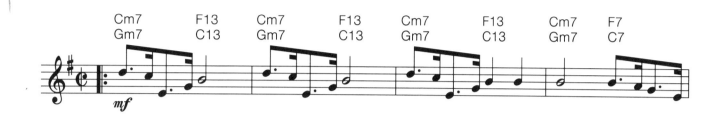

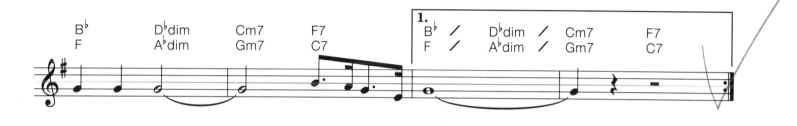

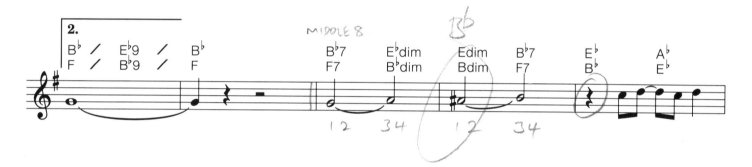

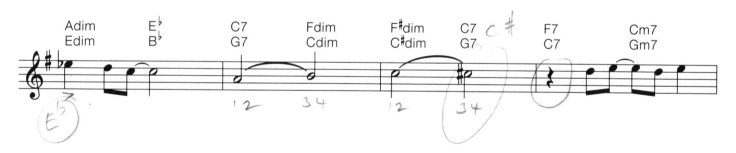

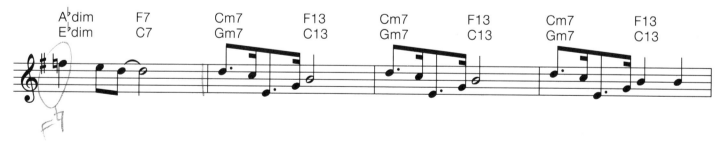

For Dancers Only

Music by Sy Oliver
Words by Don Raye & Vic Schoen

Moderate swing

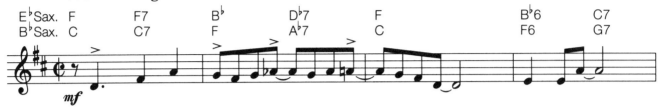

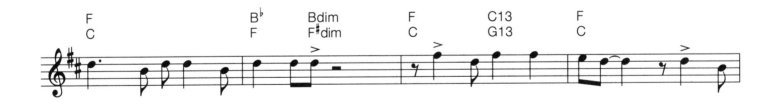

Georgia On My Mind

Words by Stuart Gorrell
Music by Hoagy Carmichael

Go Away Blues

Words & Music by Duke Ellington

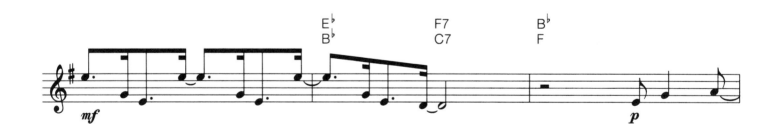

23

Hey! Ba-Ba-Re-Bop

Words & Music by Lionel Hampton & Curley Hammer

I Ain't Got Nobody (And There's Nobody Cares For Me)

Words & Music by Roger Graham & Spencer Williams

Slow drag

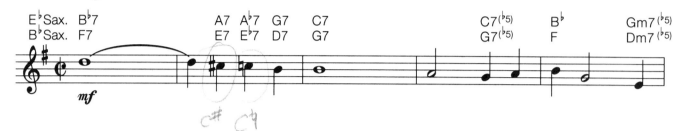

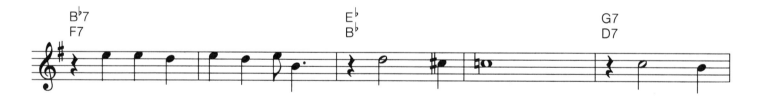

Mean To Me

Words & Music by Roy Turk & Fred E. Ahlert

I'll Remember April

Words & Music by Don Raye, Gene de Paul & Patricia Johnson

Moderato

28

The Joint is Jumpin'

Words by Andy Razaf & J. C. Johnson
Music by Thomas Waller

Lover Man (Oh Where Can You Be)

Words & Music by Jimmy Davies, Roger Ram Ramirez & Jimmy Sherman

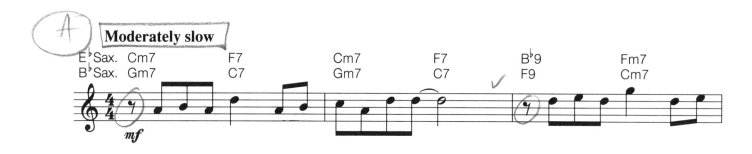

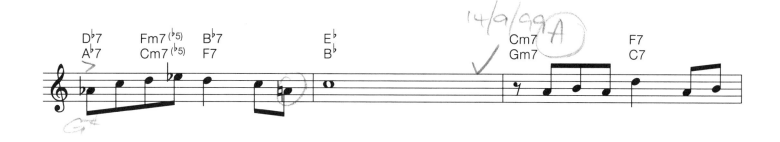

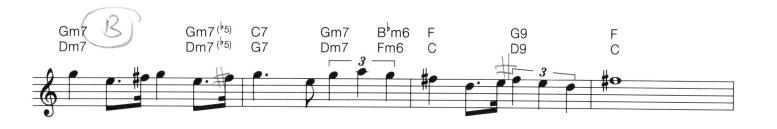

Midnight Sun

Words by Johnny Mercer
Music by Sonny Burke & Lionel Hampton

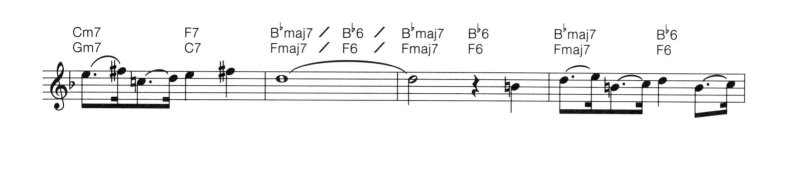

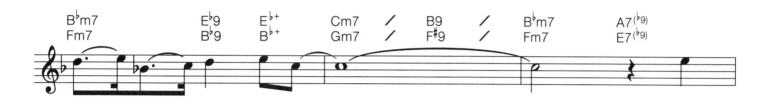

Mississippi Mud

Words & Music by Harry Barris

Mister Five By Five

Words & Music by Don Raye & Gene de Paul

Moanin'

Words by Jon Hendricks
Music by Bobby Timmons

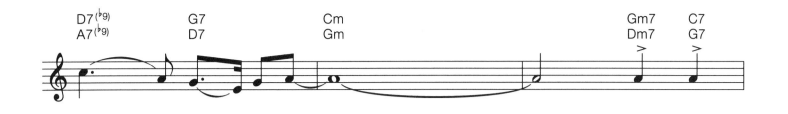

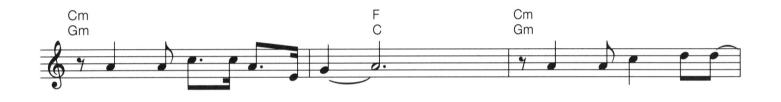

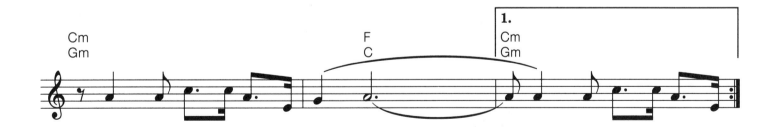

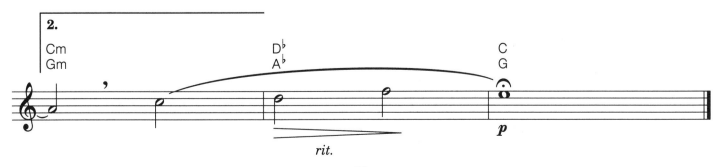

41

Mood Indigo

Words & Music by Duke Ellington, Irving Mills & Albany Bigard

Moonglow

Words & Music by Will Hudson, Eddie de Lange & Irving Mills

Moderate swing

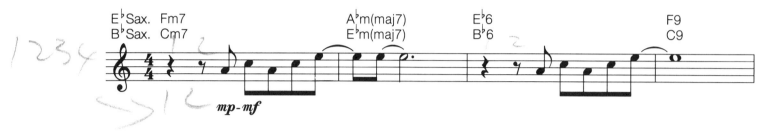

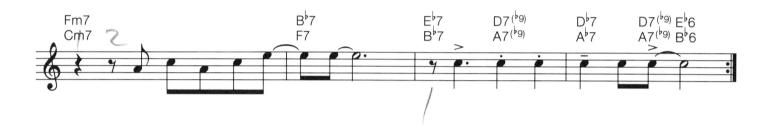

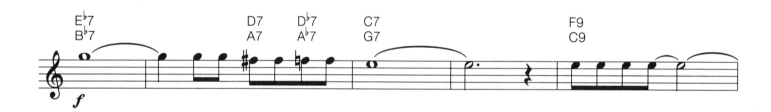

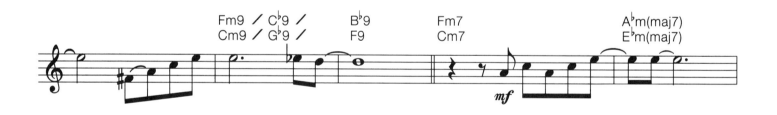

The Hawk Talks

By Louis Bellson

The Night We Called It A Day

Words by Tom Adair
Music by Matt Dennis

Slowly with expression

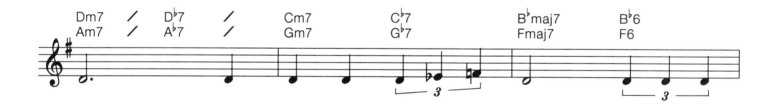

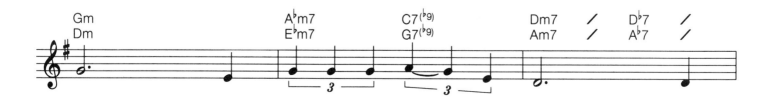

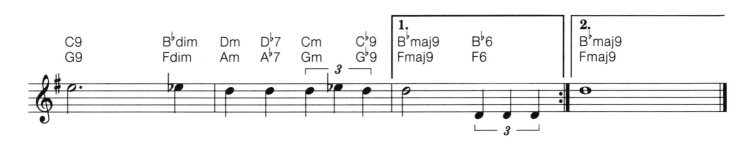

47

Perdido

Words by Harry Lenk and Ervin Drake
Music by Juan Tizol

Jump tempo

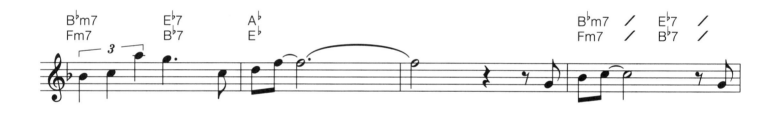

Petite Fleur (Little Flower)

Words & Music by Sydney Bechet

Satin Doll

Words by Johnny Mercer
Music by Duke Ellington & Billy Strayhorn

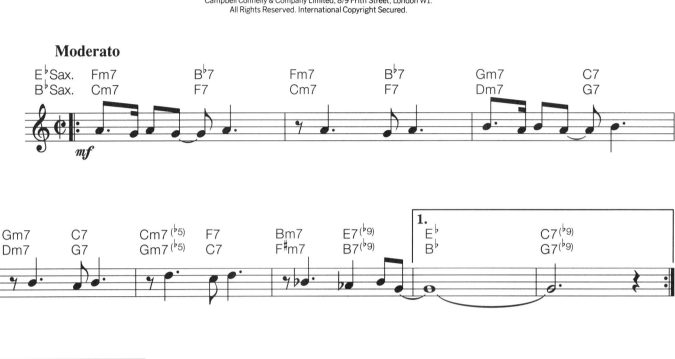

Short Stop

By Shorty Rogers

South

Words by Ray Charles
Music by Bennie Moten & T. Hayes

Moderato

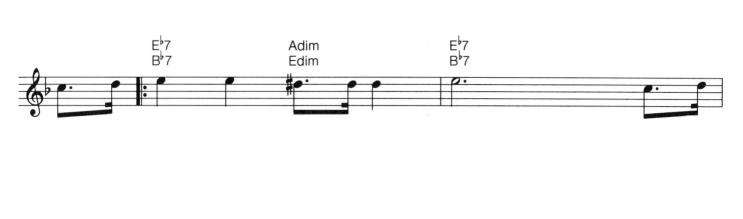

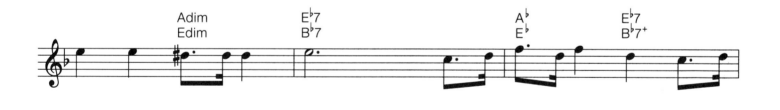

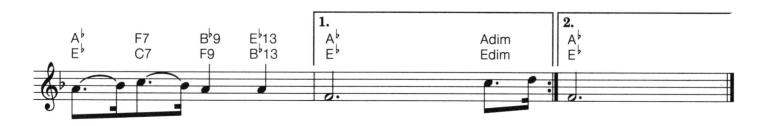

Solitude

Words by Eddie de Lange & Irving Mills
Music by Duke Ellington

Sunny

Words & Music by Bobby Hebb

T'aint What You Do (It's The Way That Cha Do It)

Words & Music by Sy Oliver & James Young

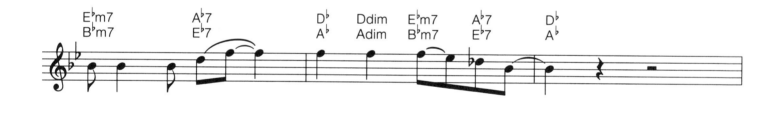

Tuxedo Junction

Words by Buddy Feyne
Music by Erskine Hawkins, William Johnson & Julian Dash

The Very Thought Of You

Words & Music by Ray Noble

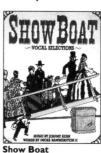